D1430296

Winter Road

Kristin Butcher

ORCA BOOK PUBLISHERS

JAN - - 2018

Library and Archives Canada Cataloguing in Publication

Butcher, Kristin, author
Winter road / Kristin Butcher.
(Orca currents)

Issued in print and electronic formats.
ISBN 978-1-4598-1550-6 (softcover).—ISBN 978-1-4598-1551-3 (PDF).—
ISBN 978-1-4598-1552-0 (EPUB)

I. Title. II. Series: Orca currents
PS8553.U6972W56 2018   jc813'.54   C2017-904486-9
C2017-904487-7

First published in the United States, 2018
Library of Congress Control Number: 2017949661

Summary: In this high-interest novel for middle readers, Kat stows away
in her mother's semitruck on a dangerous trek across a frozen lake.

*Orca Book Publishers is dedicated to preserving the environment and has
printed this book on Forest Stewardship Council® certified paper.*

Orca Book Publishers gratefully acknowledges the support for its
publishing programs provided by the following agencies: the Government
of Canada through the Canada Book Fund and the Canada Council
for the Arts, and the Province of British Columbia through
the BC Arts Council and the Book Publishing Tax Credit.

Edited by Tanya Trafford
Cover photography by Shutterstock.com
Author photo by Lisa Pedersen Photography

ORCA BOOK PUBLISHERS
www.orcabook.com

Printed and bound in Canada.

21 20 19 18 • 4 3 2 1

For Sara and Dan,
who are following their own roads.

Chapter One

I heave my bulging backpack onto the kitchen table and grin at my mother. "I'm ready if you are."

I expect her to laugh and ask if I've packed my entire closet. But she doesn't. Instead she glances uneasily at my grandmother, who isn't smiling either, so now neither am I.

"Um, about that, Kat," Mom begins but leaves her sentence hanging.

Suddenly I have a horrible feeling she is about to drop a bomb on me. The happy butterflies that have been fluttering inside my stomach all morning do a nosedive.

"About *what*?" I ask, although I'm pretty sure I don't want to know.

She takes a deep breath. "There's been a change of plans."

"What change?" The question is out before I can bite it back, and I mentally kick myself. Why do I keep asking stuff I don't want to know?

She reaches for me, but I put out my hand like a stop sign. Her arm falls to her side.

"We're not going, are we?" I say point-blank.

She reaches for me again, but I shake my head and push her hand away.

"Just tell me," I blurt, already angry, though I don't have any reason to be— yet. "Has the shipment been canceled?

Has it been given to another trucker? Are you sick? Has your rig broken down?"

"No." She shakes her head. "It's none of those things. The run is still on."

"*But*?" I wait for her to smile and tell me there is no *but*. That everything is fine. She's still taking me on this run. I'm just going to have to pack lighter. *Ha-ha. Good joke, Mom.*

So how come she's not laughing? Or smiling? Or even looking at me? She starts fidgeting with the buckles on my backpack.

"Mom!"

That makes her look up.

She sighs. "The run is still on, but there's a glitch. I was just talking to the dispatcher. He's offered me a follow-up job." She shrugs. "The payout is huge. But it means getting back to Winnipeg sooner than I planned. I can do it, but there won't be much wiggle room.

3

I know you were looking forward to coming on this trip, honey, and I know I said we'd turn it into a holiday, but if I take this second run, we won't be able to do that. There won't be time for anything but driving. You wouldn't have any fun, Kat. There'd be nothing for you to do but look out the window. You'd be bored silly."

"You said *if.*" I block out everything else my mother has said and cling to that single tiny word as if it were a life preserver keeping me afloat in a stormy sea. "*If* you take the run. That's what you said. That means you haven't accepted yet. Right?" She opens her mouth to answer, but I don't let her. "So tell the dispatcher to give the shipment to someone else. Tell him you can't do it. Because you *can't.*"

"Kat. Please." Her eyes are pleading even more than her words.

I cross my arms and shake my head stubbornly.

She bites her lip. "I'm sorry, Kat. I already told him I'd take it."

For a second, I'm so stunned I can't speak. And then I explode. "Are you serious? You took it? Really? How could you? You promised me, Mom. You *promised*! Call him back and tell him you've changed your mind."

"Katarina, stop." It's my grandmother. "Your mama, she had no choice. She—"

"Don't stick up for her, Gran," I snarl. "Of course she had a choice. She just didn't choose me." I turn away and mutter, "So what else is new?"

"Kat, I'll make it up to you. I promise."

I spin around to face her again. "Give it up, Mom. You promised I'd be going on this trip with you. Your promise is worth about as much as Monopoly money. So tell me, if you're on the road and Gran is off to Mexico, what exactly am *I* doing?"

She hangs her head and mumbles, "I've arranged for you to stay with Tina."

I throw up my hands. "Tina? Great! I get to spend my spring break with your friend, her egghead husband and their three moronic kids. Gee, thanks, Mom. You're the best. But if it's all the same to you, I'll take a pass."

I grab my backpack and jacket and run from the kitchen. I have no idea where I'm going. I'm just going. If I stay in the house, my mom and grand-mother will hunt me down, so I bolt for the front door and slam it behind me.

And then I come to a screeching halt. Now what? I look around at the dirty March snow covering the ground. It looks like I feel, and though I'm still angry, the tears start streaming down my cheeks. I swipe at them and reset my survival compass. Since Dad died eight months ago, it feels like I do that on a daily basis.

He was a trucker, which meant he was on the road a lot, so half the time it was just Mom and me holding the fort. Back then we were more than mother and daughter. We were friends. We did girl stuff—shopping, baking and painting our nails. When Dad was home, we did family things—tobogganing and skating or swimming and cycling, depending on the season.

Then my dad had a massive heart attack, and everything changed.

Now it's Mom who's on the road. She was a trucker before I was born, so the transition from stay-at-home mom to breadwinner was no big deal—for her. It was a big deal for me though. Almost faster than I could blink, my whole world got turned upside down.

We moved in with Gran, so I lost the only home I'd ever known. I had to change schools, so I lost my friends. But worst of all, I lost my family. As often as I see my mother these days, she might as well have died too.

This road trip was supposed to be our chance to find our way back to each other. I'm on spring break, so I have no school for the next ten days. But my grandmother is going on vacation in Mexico—she flies there tomorrow— which would leave me home alone. That's why Mom suggested I ride with her on her next run.

Yeah, well, so much for that. Her dispatcher snaps his fingers, and she drops me like a hot potato.

New tears spring to my eyes, and I angrily wipe them away. Do I really mean so little to my mother that she can toss me aside without a second's thought?

I choke back a sob and run down the driveway. I don't know where I'm going, but it's sure not to Tina's house.

My mom's semi—minus the trailer—is parked on the road, so I put it between me and the house, making sure to stand behind a tire so Mom and Gran won't see my feet. If they come looking for me, I want them to think I took off down the street or hid behind the house or in some shrubbery.

Sure enough, a moment later I can hear them out in the yard.

"Kat!"

"Katarina!"

As they head around the side of the house, I think about making a run for it, but then I have another idea. Last night Mom gave me a spare key to the semi for our trip—in case of an emergency, she said. Well, I'd say this situation more than qualifies. I fish the key out of my pocket and let myself into the cab of the truck as quietly as I can. Then I scrunch down in the back under all Mom's gear.

I can still hear them calling me, so I sneak a peek out the window, which is slightly open.

Mom glances at her watch. "I'm so sorry about this, Mama," she tells Gran. "I hate leaving without setting things right with Kat." She takes another look up and down the street and then checks her watch again. "But I have to get going."

Gran pats Mom's arm. "Is okay," she says and shoos Mom toward the truck. "Everything will be fine. Katarina will calm down and come home. I no leave until tomorrow. I drive her to Tina's. Don't worry. Now go."

Mom looks unsure but nods. Then she gives Gran a hug and a kiss and heads for the truck.

As I shrink back into my hiding place, excitement shoots through me like an electric current. This is not what I planned, but whether Mom likes it or not, I'm coming with her on this run.

Chapter Two

As Mom climbs into the cab, I stay perfectly still. She sticks the key into the ignition, and the motor rumbles to life, making the whole truck shake. I shake with it. It's like being on one of those vibrating motel beds, except not so comfortable. Every bolt and bump in the floor digs into me. To make matters worse, the stuff I'm hiding under suddenly weighs a ton, and I start to feel like I'm buried alive.

I've just about convinced myself I'm going to suffocate if I don't get some fresh air when Mom reaches around the seat and drops something else on top of the pile. I instantly freeze. I do not want to be discovered before we've even pulled onto the road!

I know I've only been lying here a few minutes, but it feels like hours. What's the holdup? I thought my mother was in a time crunch. *So get going already!* I scream silently at her, but several minutes later we're still idling in front of the house. Finally she buckles her seat belt, the truck grumbles into gear, and with a lurch we start to move.

Once I'm sure Mom is focused on her driving, I tunnel a hole through my little nest toward air that isn't hot and hasn't already been breathed twenty times. I hungrily suck it in, and though I'm still buried under a pile of stuff, I feel a little less claustrophobic.

I try not to think about where I am and how much I want to throw everything off and be free again. But that's easier said than done, because there's not much to distract me. Though it's broad daylight outside, I'm surrounded by darkness, unless you count the little breathing hole I've created for myself. Since it's nothing more than a periscope to the back wall of the cab, I can't see much. So I concentrate on the movement of the truck.

When it's not hauling anything, the semi has almost as much zip as a sports car, and I can tell by the smooth hum of the engine and the regular rocking motion that we're moving easily and quickly. I count the number of times we slow down and idle at intersections. As we approach number eleven, I hear the *tick, tick, tick* of the turn signal. Mom gears down. I feel the truck turning. We're moving at a crawl now, and finally we come to a complete stop. Mom switches off the engine and lets herself out of the truck.

Bang! The door slams. I wince. It's a wonder my eardrum isn't broken! I make a mental note not to position my head close to the door the next time I decide to stow away.

When I hear my mother call out to someone, I can tell she's not near the truck anymore, so I peel off the stuff covering me, sit up and look out the window. We're in a compound of container trailers. Mom is talking to some guy. I'm guessing it's the dispatcher.

It feels good to be upright. I breathe deeply and stretch. But I know I don't have much time. Already the guy is pointing to a trailer at the other end of the compound, so I quickly rearrange my little nest, moving everything hard and lumpy to the side and spreading a mattress of soft stuff on the floor. I lie down on it—with my head away from the door—and then I cover myself up again.

Just in time too. I've barely burrowed into my hiding spot when the cab door opens and Mom climbs in.

It takes about fifteen minutes to hook the trailer up, and even though there are guys out there doing most of the work, Mom hops in and out of the cab like she's a jack-in-the-box. So when the cell phone in my backpack rings, I almost freak out. Luckily, I'm hugging my backpack, so with lightning speed I reach into the compartment where I keep my phone and turn it off before it can ring again. Then I cross my fingers and pray Mom didn't hear it.

But she must have, because the first thing she does when she gets back in the semi is grab her phone. "That's odd," she mutters. "I could have sworn I heard it ring." There's a clunk as the phone lands on the dash. Mom buckles her seat belt, and we're on our way.

I sigh with relief. Another bullet dodged. I know my mom is eventually going to discover me, but hopefully by then we'll be too far away from civilization for her to do anything about it.

A couple of days ago, Mom showed me the route we would be taking, so I sort of have an idea where we're going. As long as she keeps slowing down and speeding up, I know we're still in Winnipeg. But once she hits Highway 59, it's pretty much go, go, go.

Even so, I can't believe she doesn't need a pee break. I sure do. If I'd known I was going to be hiding in the back of her truck, I would have visited the bathroom before storming out of the house. I try to estimate how far away we are from East Selkirk and hope Mom will stop there. But she keeps right on driving.

With my bladder screaming, it's all I can do to stay in my little nest, but I worry that if I pop up while she's driving, she'll be so shocked she'll lose control of the truck.

My chance comes when I least expect it. Out of nowhere, Mom pulls over and calls Gran on her phone.

"Kat still hasn't shown up?" She sounds surprised. Worried too, I think. Or maybe that's just wishful thinking on my part. "Where can she be?"

"Right here," I announce as I show myself.

Mom yelps, and though it makes my heart beat twice as fast as usual, it also makes me glad I didn't come out of hiding while she was driving.

It takes Mom a second to get herself together, but when she does, I know I'm in trouble. She glares at me as she speaks into the phone through gritted teeth. "No, I'm fine. Kat just startled me. She's here in the truck. Let me get to the bottom of this, Mama, and I'll call you back." Then she gestures to the passenger seat. I climb into it.

There's no need to go into the ugly details of what follows. Let's just say my mother isn't impressed with my sense of adventure. For starters, she grounds me until the end of twelfth grade, and that's a year and a half away! Then she says she's going to stick me on the next bus back to Winnipeg.

That's the one leaving from Pine Falls, the closest community to our present location. Except there is no bus from Pine Falls. Seems Greyhound has cut that route.

"Damn it, Kat!" Mom swears as we pull up in front of the abandoned bus terminal. She glances at her watch. "This prank of yours has already cost me forty-five minutes."

"It isn't a prank!" I protest. "You said you would take me with you. I'm just helping you keep your word."

If looks count for anything, I should be lying in a pool of blood, because Mom is definitely shooting daggers in my direction.

She takes another look at her watch and heaves an irritated sigh. "I don't have time to take you back." Then she glares at me again. "But you were probably counting on that, weren't you?"

I don't answer.

"This is not funny, Kat!" she explodes.

"I'm not laughing."

"I need this run—and the one after it."

I frown. "I know that. You told me already. I'm not asking you to change your plans. But you can't blame me for hiding in your truck. If you stop and think about it, you didn't really give me any choice. I'd rather stare out the window for two days—or five days or however many days we'll be on the road—than spend a single hour with Tina and her weird family. Ignore me the whole trip. I don't care. Anything is better than being stuck in Winnipeg."

From the way Mom's mouth drops open, I'm pretty sure she wasn't expecting me to say that. She stares out the window and raps her fingers on the steering wheel.

Finally she says, "Okay. We'll play it your way. This trip is going to be boring as hell, but if that's what you want, you've got it. I just need to know one thing."

I eye her warily. "What?"

"Do you have your insulin?"

Chapter Three

I have diabetes. I didn't have it when
Dad died—or if I did, I didn't know
it—but I definitely have it now. And as
far as I'm concerned, it's a major pain
in the butt. Not literally. I *could* take
the injections there, but mostly I stab
myself in my thigh, hip or belly with
an insulin pen. It really does look like
a pen, except there's a needle where
the nib should be. Since I take insulin

twice a day every single day, I have to keep changing the injection site, so my skin doesn't close up against the needle. Sadly, injections are now as much a part of my morning as breakfast.

Then there's the glucose meter. In a way, I hate that even more than the insulin pen, because I have to check my blood sugar four times a day! That means four times every day, I have to prick my finger and stick a blood sample into a machine to be analyzed. The reading shouldn't be too high or too low, or I could be in trouble—with my health and with Mom.

But the absolute worst part of having diabetes is that now I'm stuck on a strict diet. Not to shed pounds—my weight is fine. But sugar is my enemy. Fat too. Even carbs. That means no more cakes, cookies or chocolate bars. No French fries or potato chips either. In fact, pretty much all the things I like to eat are out.

You'd think I could have a treat once in a while, but no. My mother watches me like a hawk. There's a chart in the kitchen where I have to record when I take my insulin, and another one where I record my sugar levels. As for food, Mom writes up menus a month at a time, and there's no wavering from them. Even my grandmother—who does most of the cooking—won't cut me any slack. If I go out with my friends, my mother reminds me not to have pop or donuts or candy, and when I get home, she makes me test my blood sugar, to make sure I haven't.

So, of course, the first thing she wants to know when I show up in her truck is if I have my insulin with me. If she had her way, she'd probably make me carry it in a keg around my neck like a St. Bernard.

I roll my eyes at her. "Yes," I say. "I have my insulin *and* my glucose meter.

And no, I didn't stash any chocolate bars in my backpack." I push it toward her. "Go ahead and check it if you want."

"Why do you have to be like that, Kat?" she says. "This is your health we're talking about. And it's my job to look out for you."

"I'm sixteen, Mom! I can look out for myself!"

"Can you?" She sighs heavily. "I'm not so sure. I don't think you realize the seriousness of your condition."

"The doctor said it can be controlled."

She nods. "Yes, but not by magic. You have to follow the rules."

"Why? You follow them enough for both of us—in fact, you could be the health police for every diabetic in the world!"

Mom looks at me like she wants to argue the point but then just shakes her head, checks her mirrors for traffic and puts the truck in gear.

"I need to pee," I announce sullenly. I expect her to be ticked at me for slowing her down even more, but if she is, she doesn't show it.

"There's a gas station up the street. I'll pull in there."

The service-station washroom is gross. In fact, it's so bad, I sit on my hands instead of the toilet seat. I would cover it with toilet paper, except there isn't any. Good thing I have some tissues in my pocket. I've been in this bathroom a big three minutes, and already my skin is crawling. All I want is to wash my hands and get out. But the water is cold, the soap container is empty, and the only paper towels are crumpled on the floor. Disgusted, I wipe my hands on my jeans and head for the exit.

As I return the key to the attendant, I say, "Your washroom is out of toilet paper, soap, hot water and paper towels."

"Thanks," the woman replies, without even looking up from the magazine she's thumbing through. Clearly, the state of the bathroom is not high on her priority list. Either that or maintaining it is not part of her job description.

"Yuck!" I tell my mother as I climb back into the truck. "What a hole! That place is filthy. Did you know that?"

Mom frowns. "How could I?"

"You've driven through here before."

"Yes, but I haven't visited every public washroom. If I'd known this one was dirty, I would have gone somewhere else."

"Yeah, right," I grumble.

"What's that supposed to mean?"

"I know you're ticked at me for stowing away in your truck and putting you behind schedule."

She looks at me like I'm some sort of alien. "So you think I would punish you by sending you into a filthy bathroom? Now you're just being ridiculous," she says and pulls back onto the main road.

And just like that, I'm dismissed —again.

I look out the window. Almost before I can blink Pine Falls slides away and is quickly replaced by trees, sky and a road that leads off into eternity. It's like a boring video that keeps playing over and over. There's not even a dead skunk on the highway to break up the monotony. I know I said I'd rather stare out the window for days than be stuck in Winnipeg with Tina, but I didn't really think it would happen.

I can't admit that to my mother though. She'd say, *I told you so*, and with everything else that's gone wrong in my life lately, I don't need that.

I pull out my phone and check the time. It's ten fourteen. I groan. We've been on the road for barely an hour and a half, and already this trip is agony.

I can't believe I was actually looking forward to it. I'd been so sure it was going to be fun—something for Mom and me to do together. The two of us talking and laughing, being silly, sharing our thoughts and dreams—just like we used to.

I glance across the cab at her. She's close enough to touch, so how come she feels so far away?

All the anger and hurt I've been holding inside for the past eight months comes bubbling to the surface. My life used to be so good, and now it's horrible. I hate it! I'm mad at my dad for dying. I'm mad at my body for breaking down, and I'm mad at my mother for abandoning me when I really need her.

I'm just about to break down and start blubbering when Mom's phone rings, startling me out of my pity party.

"Hello," she says, never once taking her eyes off the road. She doesn't need to, because her phone is hooked into the truck's Bluetooth. All she has to do is hit a button on the steering wheel to make the connection.

"Hey, Iron Maiden, how's it going? Long time no see."

Mom laughs. "Oh my gosh! Nobody has called me that in years. Harvey Dickinson, is that you? How *are* you?"

I check the screen on Mom's phone. She's right. It *is* Harvey Dickinson, whoever he is.

"I'm good," he says.

"And Mandy?"

"She's good too. Holding the fort with the kids."

"Uh-huh," Mom says. "So what's up? How'd you get my number?"

"I was talking with your dispatcher."

"You know Charlie?"

"Oh yeah. He and I go way back. Anyway, I'd heard you were driving again, and since I knew Dave had driven for Charlie, I played a hunch."

"Well, if I recall correctly, your hunches were always pretty good. I take it you're still terrorizing the highways." Even if I can't see the big smile on my mother's face, I can hear it in her voice.

"I do what I can. Got my own company in Saskatoon now. I'm breaking in a rookie as we speak. He's driving, and I'm sitting back with my feet up."

They both laugh.

"I understand you're hauling a load up the winter road, east of Bloodvein," Harvey says.

"Yes. I have a shipment for Pauingassi."

"That's what I heard. As it turns out, I'm heading up there myself—as far as Little Grand Rapids anyway."

"No kidding," Mom says. "Small world."

"Anyway, based on when Charlie said you picked up your load, I'm thinking you're not far behind me."

"I turned onto the 304 about twenty minutes ago," Mom tells him.

"Excellent." Harvey chuckles. "What say we meet up for lunch in about an hour? I'll wait for you at that truck stop on the hill about halfway along the highway. You know the one."

Mom nods even though he can't see her. "I do. See you then."

When the phone disconnects, I lean forward and peer at my mother. "Iron Maiden?"

She looks embarrassed. "It was my CB handle back in the day."

"How the heck did you get a name like Iron Maiden? No, wait. On second thought, I don't want to know. I might end up scarred for life."

Chapter Four

Mom laughs. I don't. I want to, and a few months ago I would have. But now it's like my mother and I are standing on opposite sides of the Grand Canyon. If I laughed, I would be saying everything is okay when it isn't.

"Why did you become a trucker anyway?" I sneer.

Her laugh dries up. "It seemed like a good idea at the time." Her voice is flat.

"I'd graduated from university, and after four months of job hunting, I still hadn't found anything. So much for a commerce degree. Since my father was hinting it was time I moved out, and I had a pile of student loans to pay off, I was getting desperate. So when I saw an advertisement for tractor-trailer drivers, I jumped at it." She shrugs. "It meant forking out more money for driving lessons, but I figured it would be worth the investment in the long run."

"Isn't that a bit extreme?" I ask as if I am the parent and she is the kid. "I mean, you could've taken a job in a store or a restaurant."

"Oh, Kat," she mutters under her breath. "If I'd done that, I'd *still* be paying off my student loans. Long-distance driving pays a lot better."

"So marrying a trucker helped pay your bills."

Mom's mouth drops open. "What an awful thing to say!"

"Hey, you just admitted you needed to pay off your student loans," I remind her. "And Dad *was* a trucker. And he was ten years older than you, so he probably already had some money."

"For your information, your father did not pay off my student loans!" Mom huffs. "I did that myself, thank you very much."

I roll my eyes. "Whatever." I go back to staring out the window.

After a few minutes, Mom sighs. "Those early days were good though. I enjoyed driving more than I thought I would. It gave me a lot of time to think."

"If you enjoyed it so much, why'd you give it up?" I practically spit out the words.

Mom's voice hardens. "Because I became pregnant with you."

"So you're saying I was an accident."

Mom slams her hand on the steering wheel. "Damn it, Kat! What in the world is wrong with you?" Her words bounce off the walls of the cab. "I'm not saying that at all! In fact, you were very much planned. Why are you being such a little witch this morning? It's like you're looking for a fight."

She's right. I am, though I'm not sure why. Maybe I want my mother to hurt as much as I do. Maybe I'm so desperate to connect with her, even a fight would feel good. Or maybe I just need to vent the frustration and anger that's been building since my dad died. Who knows? Maybe it's all those things.

At any rate, emotions swell inside me like a tidal wave. If I open my mouth to speak, I know they'll come pouring out, so I blink back the hot tears stinging my eyes and turn to the window once more.

But my mother knows me too well.

"Come on, kiddo," she says softly. "I know something's wrong. And it's more than the last-minute change of plans. Tell me what's bugging you."

I don't say anything. I can't. My throat is swollen shut. I can't even swallow, never mind speak. But somehow a sob gets past the boulder lodged in my throat.

"Oh, honey," my mother says in a way that reminds me of my old mom, the one who used to send me off to school with a kiss and a wave every morning, the one who took me to get my ears pierced, the one who laughed at my dumb jokes.

All the memories of life the way it used to be come flooding back and swamp me. And suddenly I'm bawling like a baby. Why did everything have to change?

Mom pulls over to the side of the highway, slips the semi into neutral and sets the brake. Then she unbuckles her seat belt, and the next thing I know, she's swallowed me up in her arms. I instantly melt.

"I'm right here, baby," she says, stroking my hair. "Tell me what's bothering you. Whatever it is, we'll figure it out."

I shake my head and whimper into her shoulder, "We can't."

She tries to console me. "Of course we can."

I push away from her and swipe at my tears with the heel of my hand. "How?" I demand. "I can't bring Dad back. Can you?"

She shuts her eyes and shakes her head. "I miss him too, Kat."

"It's not just that!" I wail and grab a tissue from the box on the console. I blow my nose before continuing. "It's everything else too."

"You mean the diabetes?" Mom says.

"All of it! My whole life! Don't you see?" I wave my arms in frustration. "Our house is gone. I had to change schools, so I never see my friends anymore." I pause before adding, "And I almost never see you. You're always on the road. We never talk or do things together. It's like you ran away when Dad died."

Mom tears up, and her chin starts to quiver. "Oh, Kat, I know it's not like it used to be, but you're not alone, honey. When I'm away, you have Gran."

I shake my head again and frown. "It's not the same. I love Gran, but she's not you. Why can't you stay home like you used to?"

"Oh, honey, I wish I could. I miss our times together too. But I have no choice. I have to make a living."

"I get that, but why do you have to do it driving truck? Couldn't you get a job in Winnipeg?"

She sighs heavily. "Not doing anything that pays as well."

"What if we spent less money?" It seems like an obvious solution to me. "Scrap my allowance. I'll give up my cell phone. Cancel the cable. I'll get a library card. Whatever we need to do, let's do it. Please, Mom. I just want you home."

She squeezes my hand and tries to smile. "If only it were that simple." Then she looks around the cab of the semi. "This truck is only a year old. Your father bought it brand new. I have to pay for it, and that's a lot of money."

"So sell it," I say.

"I'll never get its full value. I'd still have a huge debt but no truck. Then there's all the other everyday costs of living—rent, food, insurance, clothes, saving for university and a hundred other expenses."

Just when I thought we were making progress, we crash into another wall. I start to close up again. "So you're saying you won't find a different job."

"I'm saying I *can't*—at least not until I pay off the truck."

I give it one more shot. "What if I got a part-time job?"

Mom smiles sadly. "Not only do I not want that for you, but it wouldn't help much, I'm afraid. Still, I love you for offering."

"You see," I say, giving up. "I told you we couldn't figure it out."

She shakes her head. "You're wrong. Recognizing the problem is a start." She sighs. "To tell you the truth, I guess I have pulled away since your dad died— without realizing it. I've been so focused on making everything work—earning a living, staying on top of your diabetes and trying not to burden you with how much I miss your dad—that I haven't thought enough about what you're going through.

"I *have to* work, Kat, and for now that means driving truck. But it won't be forever—I swear. In the meantime we have to make the most of the time we *do* have. What do you say? I'll try if you will."

I want that more than anything, though I have my doubts, so I nod and smile, but I also tear up again.

That's all it takes for Mom to get choked, and when our hands collide reaching for tissues, we both laugh.

She climbs back into her seat and dabs at her eyes. "If I'm going to drive, I need to see the road."

"Yup," I say. "That would be good."

Chapter Five

Since truckers keep crazy hours, truck stops are open twenty-four/seven. Food might not be served the whole time, but drivers can always gas up and have a shower. So there's usually a few tractor-trailers around. But when Mom and I pull off Highway 304 to have lunch with Harvey Dickinson, there are so many semis in the parking lot, you'd think we were at a trucking convention. The sun is shining, and despite the snow it feels more like May than March, so I leave my jacket in the truck.

Needless to say, the restaurant is packed. Harvey must've been watching for Mom, though, because as soon as we step inside, a guy at a booth across the room starts waving his arms like the starter at the Indy 500.

I nudge Mom with my elbow and nod toward him. "Looks like you've still got it, Iron Maiden," I tease. "Or else that's your friend."

My mother actually blushes. "Enough with the Iron Maiden cracks."

I nod obediently. "Whatever you say. Should I call you Donna then? You could say I'm your younger sister."

Mom glares at me. "Don't be cute, Kat. Call me what you always call me."

"To your face or behind your back?" I try to look innocent.

She rolls her eyes, then grabs my arm and starts pulling me across the room. Into my ear she whispers, "Embarrass me in front of Harvey, and I'll switch your shampoo with white glue—I swear."

"That should take care of my flyaway hair," I mutter and then snicker at my own joke.

Though she tries to keep a straight face, Mom chuckles too, and by the time we reach the booth, we're both outright laughing.

The man stands, and suddenly I'm looking straight up. He has to be nearly seven feet tall. Mom's no midget, and even though she's on tiptoe, he still has to double over to hug her.

When he finally lets her go and steps back, I can see another guy sitting at the booth—a young guy, and he's totally hot! I hadn't really been looking forward to this lunch, but suddenly I'm thinking it might not be too bad.

When the guy smiles, I realize I'm staring. I smile back self-consciously and then look around the room like somebody called my name. And then somebody does.

"Harvey, I'd like you to meet my daughter, Kat."

He smiles and sticks out his hand. It's huge.

"Nice to meet you," I say, watching in awe as his fingers swallow mine—halfway up to my elbow!

"It's a pleasure," he replies gallantly, releasing my hand and turning toward the guy in the booth.

"Ladies, I'd like you to meet Finn Fergus, my newest driver. Finn, this is my old friend, Donna Mulholland, and her daughter, Kat."

"Hey." Finn nods and smiles.

Mom smiles back. "Hello, Finn. Nice to meet you."

"Hi," I mumble.

Harvey gestures toward the booth. Mom slides in, and Harvey sits down beside her. Since there's only one spot left, I ease myself onto the vinyl bench beside Finn.

The menus are already on the table, so Mom and I open ours. Finn and Harvey don't.

Mom looks up. "Have you guys already ordered?"

Harvey shakes his head. "Nah, but we've had plenty of time to decide what we want."

I glance at Finn. "So what are you having?"

"A burger and fries." Then he taps the glass on the table in front of him. "And a Coke."

"Yeah, that sounds good," I say and start to close the menu.

"Oh, look at this, Kat." Mom holds up her menu and points to a photo. All I can see is the glare of the restaurant's fluorescent lights bouncing off the glossy laminated page.

"What is it?" I ask, though I'd bet anything that whatever she's found isn't nearly as appetizing as a hamburger.

"A grilled chicken breast on a bed of linguine in red-pepper sauce. It makes my mouth water just reading the description. Let's have that."

From the perky tone of Mom's voice and the sparkly expression on her face, a person would think she really wanted that. But I'm not fooled for a second. The only reason she's pointed it out is because it's a diabetes-friendly dish. And though it might sound like she's offering me a suggestion, she's really telling me what to order. I don't have a choice, and I know it.

"Yeah," I say. "Sure. Let's get that."

Mom smiles. Message sent and received. Mission accomplished.

When the server comes, Mom places our order. Whole-wheat pasta, cooked *al dente*, and as a special bonus, I get a glass of milk. I would do cartwheels, but the restaurant is crowded.

Mom and Harvey are totally consumed with their memories, leaving no room—or interest—for Finn and me.

"So how long have you been driving truck?" I ask Finn as we wait for our lunch.

He shrugs. "A couple of months."

"Why?" I say.

His eyebrows bunch up in confusion. "What do you mean?"

"Why did you choose trucking? There are a lot of other jobs out there."

"I guess. But you have to work at something. Why not trucking?"

"'Cause you're never home?"

"That's not really an issue," he replies.

"So you're not married?"

He snorts and sends me an *are you nuts* look.

"Okay," I say, "but someday you probably will be. My dad was a trucker, and he was away from home almost as much as he was around. It made it tough to be a family."

He shrugs. "Your mom is a trucker too."

"Yeah, but she stopped when I was born and only started driving again after my dad died." I steal a glance at my mom and Harvey and lower my voice. "And it's already causing problems. Trust me. Trucking is not a family-friendly occupation."

Finn grins. "I'll keep that in mind if I ever decide to get married and have kids."

Suddenly I feel self-conscious, like maybe I'm getting too personal.

I change the subject. "Have you ever driven the winter road before?"

He shakes his head. "Nope. This is my first time. That's why Harvey's bringing me on this run—to show me the ropes."

"Aren't you nervous about crashing through the ice?" I ask. "You're going to be driving a thirty-thousand-kilo tractor-trailer onto a lake."

"A winter lake," he reminds me. "The ice is really thick."

"Yeah, but it's getting to be spring. You can already feel the heat in the sun."

Harvey joins our conversation. "And it's supposed to get warmer. Still, there's not much chance of going through the ice. The authorities keep a close eye on things. They'll shut down the winter roads if they think they're unsafe. The worst that would happen is that they'd close them while we're in the boonies."

I immediately think about how my mom has to get back to Winnipeg for her other run. Getting stranded would not be good.

Mom swats Harvey's arm. "Scare the pants off her, why don't you?" she scolds. "You don't need to worry about making it back home, Kat," she says, turning to me. "We're doing a quick turnaround, and even with the warm weather, the ice won't break down that quickly."

The server arrives with our food, and I look longingly at Finn's burger and fries.

"Want some?" he asks.

Across the table, Mom raises a warning eyebrow.

"No, thanks," I say as I stab my fork into my chicken.

Now the main sounds are the *clunk* and *clink* of dishes and cutlery. After a while, though, I find myself listening to the truckers in the booth behind me.

One guy is doing most of the talking—
bragging, actually. From what I can
gather, he has a new truck—the best one
on the road, according to him.

"How is it on diesel?" someone asks.

"I'm getting nearly 15 k. per liter,"
he says.

"No way!" another guy scoffs. "Now
I know you're lying. No rig gets that
kind of mileage."

"This one does, man."

"Yeah, going downhill maybe."

They all laugh.

"And it really moves, even when I'm
hauling. Speaking of which, I gotta get
going. See you, gents."

As he passes our table, he nods to
Finn.

"You know that blowhard?" Harvey
asks. Clearly, he was listening to the
conversation too.

"Sort of," Finn replies. "His name
Dwayne Bradley. We were in driving

school together. He's not so bad really. He talks a good story, but he's okay."

"And he's got his own rig?" Mom says. "How? He's just a kid. Where would he get that kind of money?"

Finn shoves a couple of fries into his mouth. "His dad's got a few bucks, and Dwayne's an only child. His old man buys him just about anything he wants."

"Too bad," Mom mutters, turning back to her lunch. "He might be less obnoxious if he had to struggle a bit."

Chapter Six

Lunch is over before I know it. The thing is, I don't want it to end. Finn and I are just starting to get to know each other.

"Maybe we'll see you around," he says as I slide out of the booth.

I smile. "Yeah, probably—considering we're headed in the same direction." I think about giving him my phone number, but he didn't ask for it. And with Mom and Harvey right there, it would be embarrassing to offer it. Besides, Finn's a smart guy. If he wants to look me up, he'll figure it out.

"He's too old for you," Mom says as we climb into the truck.

I screw up my face like I don't know what she's talking about.

She laughs. "Don't play innocent with me, Katarina Mulholland. I'm your mother, remember? You think I didn't see you flirting with that young man?"

"Finn," I say. "His name is Finn. And I wasn't flirting."

Mom rolls her eyes. "Fine. Finn. And yes, you were. It's been a while since I've done any dating, but I still recognize the dance."

"Honestly, Mother." I shake my head. "You've been reading too many romance novels."

She laughs again and starts up the truck. "Nice try, kiddo."

"We had lunch," I protest. "That's all. Arranged by you and Harvey, I might add. Finn and I had no say in the matter. So we talked. It was either that or stare at our plates while you and Harvey strolled down memory lane."

But Mom isn't about to be led off topic. "He's too old for you, so you might as well forget about him right now."

"He's twenty-three," I say.

"And you're sixteen. That's seven years. I rest my case."

"I'll be seventeen in two months, so it's really only six years," I point out. "And besides, Dad was ten years older than you."

For a few seconds she doesn't answer. I'm not sure if it's because I just cut her argument to ribbons or because she's concentrating on maneuvering the semi out of the parking lot.

"You don't know anything about him," she says when we're finally on the highway.

"Jeez, Mother!" I grumble. "You're acting like I want to marry the guy. I just met him. But I like him, and I wouldn't mind getting to know him better. What's wrong with that?"

Mom reverts to her original objection. "He's too old for you."

I growl through my teeth, "Explain to me how Dad wasn't too old for you, but Finn is too old for me. When you were my age, Dad would've been twenty-six."

"Yes, but I wasn't a minor when I met your father. I was a grown woman. I was twenty-two."

"Twenty-two. Wow. Just about ready to collect a pension," I say, and despite her determination to play the mother card and squash my friendship with Finn before it even gets started, she laughs. So I do too. Then I remind her that twenty-two isn't that much older than almost seventeen. "In a little over a year, I'll be eighteen, Mom—aka an adult. Or, as you put it, *a grown woman*."

Zing! Got her again.

I have to hand it to my mother. She doesn't give up easily. "Age differences are tricky. A few years is a huge gap when you're young but less noticeable as you get older—which you aren't. If you were two and Finn was eight, you would not be hanging out together. Your worlds would be too different. You'd have nothing in common. But when he's fifty and you're forty-four, the six years will be nothing."

My jaw drops open, and I stare at her. "Are you saying I have to wait until I'm in my forties before I can hang out with him?"

"Okay, okay. Truce," she says, chuckling. "We'll talk about it when and if it becomes an issue."

"Deal," I agree. At the moment, this is as close as my mother is going to come to giving in, but it's a start. And she's right about one thing. If I never see Finn again, we could be arguing about nothing. I guess time will tell. In a way, though, it would be kind of cool if something did develop between us— kind of like an echo of my parents. Finn is a trucker, my dad was a trucker. Finn is older than me, Dad was older than my mom. Finn is good-looking and seems like a nice guy, and my dad was too. That's when it hits me. Maybe *that's* why my mother doesn't want Finn and me to get together. He reminds her of my father, and that must hurt, because Dad's gone.

"So tell me how you knew Dad was the one," I say.

Mom sighs. "It was more a case of ruling out reasons why he was *not* the one. We went out for a couple of years before we got married, and in that whole time I couldn't find anything about him that sounded alarm bells."

"How romantic," I say. "Did you have a checklist?"

"No. Of course not. It's just that I'd been in a relationship before I met your dad, and for a while I'd thought that guy was Mr. Right. But as soon as we got engaged, things started to go sour. Things he said and did that I'd originally thought were cute little personality quirks really started to bother me. I guess it was the same for him, and as soon as we graduated from university, he went his way and I went mine. So when I met your father, I was a bit more wary."

I swivel toward her. "You never told me you were engaged to someone before Dad."

She shrugs. "It never came up."

"Did Dad know?"

She laughs. "Of course he knew. Just like I knew about his past relationships."

"Dad had other girlfriends before you?"

Mom smirks. "He was in his thirties when we met, so what do you think?"

"Huh." I have to admit, the idea blows my mind a little. In fact, I couldn't be more surprised if Mom said she'd been a secret agent.

As I try to get my head around this new version of my parents, I stare absently out the window. In the distance, on the side of the highway, a semi hauling a long flatbed piled with lumber has its flashers blinking.

Mom sees it too. "I wonder if there's a problem," she says. She slows down and pulls up beside the other truck. It's shiny red, and the chrome on it gleams like there's a force field between it and the dirty snow. Mom hits a button, and the window on my side opens.

Now I can see the driver. It's the blowhard guy from the truck stop. He looks like he's sleeping.

Mom honks her horn and leans toward the open window. The guy jumps and rolls down his window.

"Everything okay?" Mom asks.

The guys smiles. "Yeah. It's all good. I was just taking care of some paperwork."

With your eyes closed? I think. *And on the side of the highway? Why didn't you take care of it in the parking lot, before you got moving?*

"No mechanical trouble?" Mom says.

"With this baby?" The guy is all bravado again. He runs his hand proudly over the steering wheel. "There better not be. She's brand new."

Mom waves. "Okay then. If you're sure. Drive safe." Then she does up the window, slips the truck into gear, and we're off again.

"He wasn't doing paperwork," I say.

Mom shakes her head. "I didn't think so either."

"He was sleeping."

She shrugs. "All I know is that he didn't look too good. I wonder if he's sick."

"If he is, why didn't he say so?"

Mom looks at me and raises an eyebrow. "A big tough guy like him? It would tarnish his image."

"That's dumb."

"Yes, it is."

"We might have been able to help him."

"Clearly he didn't want help, Kat. Some people are like that. Too much pride for their own good." She pauses and then says, "It's time to check your sugar levels. Don't forget to record the reading."

How convenient of my mother to remember my diabetes right at this moment. But unless I want to look like Dwayne, the ego-trip trucker, I can't argue. Coincidence? I don't think so. And when I see the corners of Mom's mouth fighting back a smile, I know so.

Chapter Seven

Highway 304 is completely clear during our drive north, so we make pretty good time. Until we move onto a gravel road riddled with potholes. Of course, Mom slows right down, but even with my seat belt on, I bounce all over the place. When we get to Bloodvein and hang a right onto a narrow track of packed snow, we slow down even more. I check out the speedometer. Fifteen kilometers an hour—that's it! I could walk faster.

"Why are we going so slow?" I ask.

"This is a winter road," Mom says. "It only exists a couple of months a year. When the snow melts, the road is gone. It'll take us where we need to go, but it's fragile, especially under the weight of a big truck. Driving slow is less likely to compromise it."

We're soon deep into the bush, and though the sky is still blue, the sun is lower, and its rays are playing hide-and-seek among the trees. Since the truck takes up practically the whole road, I can't help wondering what we'll do if we meet a vehicle coming the other way. But I know this isn't Mom's first trip over a winter road, which means she's probably run into the situation before. So there's no point in my worrying about it.

Crossing rivers, on the other hand, does make me worry, especially since there are quite a few. It's not that they're superwide, but the semi has to go down a bank to get onto them and then climb another on the other side to get back onto land. Mom says bridges have been built over many of the rivers on other winter roads, but that doesn't help us, and I hold my breath with each crossing.

The scariest section of the road, though, is a spot called Webster's Corner, a sharp right turn on the slippery road. Mom says more than one semi has overturned here. I hang on to the door and hold my breath until we're past it.

It's six o'clock when we get to Round Lake, and though it's almost dark, Mom decides to put chains on. I offer to help—not that I know what to do—but she says she can handle it. Besides, she wants me to eat. There are prepared meals in the cab's mini fridge, so I heat one in the microwave and hungrily wolf it down.

When I'm done, I get out of the truck to stretch my legs. Without the sun to warm things up, it feels like winter again, so I zip my jacket, pull up my hood and stuff my hands into my pockets.

Mom has already retrieved the chains from the rack where they hang when not in use and has draped them over the outside tires. She moves the truck backward and forward to get the chains in the right position to lock.

"How come you don't put them on all the tires?" I ask.

"I need traction, but I don't want to chew up the ice. It's a fine line. Some truckers don't use chains at all."

It takes Mom a half hour or so to get the chains the way she wants them.

After a while I lose interest and turn toward the lake. The truck's headlights cast an eerie beam over the ice road that runs from the shore out into the darkness. Mom says the crossing is about three kilometers. I know truckers drive it every winter without anything going wrong, but temperatures have been higher than normal lately, so I keep picturing us getting halfway across and crashing through the ice.

Finished with the chains, Mom walks out onto the lake and peers closely at the edge where ice and land meet. I look too. There's a layer of slush on top of the ice. She slides her foot through it, then moves farther out and jumps a few times.

"Should be okay," she finally says.

"*Should be*?" I echo anxiously.

She smiles. "Don't worry, sweetie. I wouldn't attempt to drive on it if I thought it was unsafe." She hops back to shore and links her arm through mine. "So let's get going. I want to make Pauingassi tonight, and we've still got a long way to go."

When I climb back into the truck, my entire body is clenched. I'm not sure if that's from bracing myself against the cold or because I'm nervous about driving on the lake. Despite Mom's assurances, I'm still worried. The truck could break down, we could hit a weak spot in the ice, or we could run into bad weather. And it's not like we can call a tow truck to rescue us. We're in the middle of nowhere.

"Don't buckle up," Mom says, when I reach for my seat belt. "And open your window. Just to be safe. Nothing is going to happen, but we want to be able to exit the truck quickly—if we have to."

My head whips round toward her, and my stomach does a couple of somersaults. *Everything is fine, but get ready to bail.* Talk about mixed messages. If my mother is trying to put me at ease, she's not succeeding. "Right," I mutter as I let go of my seat belt. Then I roll down my window and grab hold of the door.

As the truck moves onto the frozen lake, I hold my breath and wait for us to plunge through the ice. *If we're going down, please let it be while we're still close enough to make it back to shore.*

I keep one eye on the ice road and the other on the side mirror, and even though it's too dark to see anything, I mentally cling to the memory of land behind us.

As we push on into the night, I feel like I'm in a *Star Trek* movie. Except for the light thrown by the semi's headlights, we're surrounded by darkness and boldly going where no one has gone before. Well, at least we're going where *I* haven't gone before. As we crawl through the darkness, the ice road shows itself a bit at a time, appearing ahead of us and then disappearing behind, adding to my sense of floating in space.

The ice road is many times wider than the snow road, but we drive down the center of it, well away from the snowbanks that define its boundaries. When I ask why, Mom says the windrows—that's trucker talk for snowbanks—weaken the ice.

"So why have them?" I ask.

"They guide us across the lake, for one thing," she says, "and they help keep blowing snow from drifting onto the road."

It has started to get foggy, almost like steam rising off the lake, so visibility is getting to be an issue. If anything,

Mom drives slower than ever, but she doesn't stop. Even I know stopping is a big no-no on an ice road. The concentrated weight of a loaded truck in one spot can cause the ice to give out. As it is, it's groaning and popping, which does nothing to relieve my anxiety.

I had expected the road to head straight across the lake, but it actually veers right. As we make the slight turn, the lights of a vehicle coming up behind us reflect in the mirror on my side of the truck. The fact that the vehicle is getting closer tells me it's traveling way faster than we are, and soon it's right on our tail. It's another semi.

The blare of its horn rips the night, setting my heart thumping madly in my chest.

"What the—" Mom growls, splitting her attention between the road and her rearview mirror. "What the hell is this guy playing at? Is he crazy? He's way too close. And he's moving way too fast. Is he trying to kill us all?"

I sure hope not, but I don't say anything. I'm pretty sure my mom isn't expecting an answer.

The horn sounds again—longer this time. And then a third time.

"What is your problem, jerk?" she yells at her rearview mirror.

"I think he's going to pass," I say.

"Only an idiot would pass on an ice road if he didn't have to."

"Maybe he does."

Mom doesn't answer. She just keeps driving and checking her mirror.

But the guy doesn't back off, and he's soon even with us and traveling fast for being on an ice road. In a few seconds he barrels past. Then all I can see are his taillights.

"Hang on!" There's alarm in Mom's voice, so I do what she says, though I don't know why.

And then I do. Within seconds, the ice starts to heave and roll under us like we're on a water bed.

"What is that?" I scream, getting set to jump out of the truck.

"Hang on!" Mom says again. "Don't panic." I notice she's gripping the steering wheel as tightly as I am the door. "That idiot trucker set off a mini tidal wave under the ice."

"What?" I scream again.

"Stay calm," she says through gritted teeth. "If we need to abandon the truck, I'll let you know." After what feels like forever but is probably less than a minute, she takes a deep breath and lets it out slowly. "I think we're okay."

Hopefully, she's right. The ice does seem to have stopped moving, though

I'm not yet willing to let go of the door handle. As I watch the shiny red semi disappear into the fog ahead, I start to shake.

Chapter Eight

We roll into Little Grand Rapids around midnight. Mom's original plan was to carry on to Pauingassi, but she changes her mind and calls it a day. I think she's as freaked out about what happened out on the lake as I am.

"You need your sleep," she says.

I *am* tired, but I feel guilty about putting her behind schedule. If she weren't concerned about me, she'd probably push on.

Little Grand Rapids has shut down for the night, so we park the truck—leaving the motor running so we don't freeze—and crawl into a skinny double bed that pulls down from the back wall of the cab. It's definitely cramped quarters, but I guess I'm not too particular, because I'm dead to the world in a matter of seconds.

I would probably sleep around the clock, except Mom doesn't let me.

"Come on, Sleeping Beauty." She pokes me.

Since it's just as dark as when I closed my eyes, I can't help wondering if it's still night.

She nudges me again. "We have to get moving. Wash your face and take your insulin. I've put out some breakfast for you."

So it is morning. *Darn.* I could use more sleep. Nevertheless, I push myself to a sitting position, stretch and yawn. "What time is it?"

"Almost six. If we hit the road in the next fifteen minutes, we can make Pauingassi by eight and be back in Winnipeg tonight. It'll be another long day, but at least we'll be on track again."

"Hey, look." I squint out the window and point to a semi on the other side of the parking lot. "I'm pretty sure that wasn't here last night."

"It's Harvey and Finn," Mom says. She waves a piece of paper at me. "They left us a note. They want to meet up at the truck stop again on the way back."

"Will there be time?" I feel my hopes climb.

She shakes her head. "I left a reply on their windshield with our regrets."

Rats! I think, though I don't say anything. But just in case my disappointment shows in my face, I lower my head and start rummaging through my backpack for my insulin.

Pauingassi is pretty much like Little Grand Rapids but a third the size. Simple wood-sided buildings huddle together in sparse clearings. There are no gas stations, high-rises or fast-food joints. No movie theaters, neon signs or bustling shops. The biggest structure is the school. I'm astounded that anyone even tries to live in this place. It's way too barren and remote for me. Cell phones don't even work. I could never survive here, and yet hundreds of people are doing exactly that.

"It's so bleak and desolate," I say. "Why would people want to live somewhere like this? How do they earn a living?"

Mom shrugs. "They hunt and fish and harvest wild rice. And they help build the winter roads each year."

"That's it?"

She nods. "It's a hard life by our standards for sure, but these people value a oneness with nature and the elements. It's a cultural thing."

"Okay, but they still need food and clothes and fuel for their homes," I point out. "How do they get supplies when there's no winter road?"

"Not easily," she says. "Helicopters, floatplanes and boats are their only links to the rest of Manitoba during the warmer months. They can get the basics but not the big things."

I think about what that must be like as we pull up to the only store in Pauingassi and park beside a shiny red semi.

Mom instantly begins to mutter. "It's that jackass from the truck stop— the same moron who caused the ice roll on Round Lake. I'm going to tear such a strip off him, he's not going to know what hit him. He won't be messing with me again anytime soon."

Having lived with my mother for nearly seventeen years, I have no doubt she means what she says. I almost feel sorry for the guy.

When we hop out of the truck and head inside to announce ourselves to the storekeeper, who should we bump into but Dwayne Bradley, owner of the red semi. He's carrying a thermos—of coffee, I assume, since he looks like he hasn't slept.

"Hey," he grins. "Fancy meeting you ladies in this tropical paradise. Looks like it's going to be another warm day. I hope you brought your swimsuits. Don't lounge around too long though.

You might not get back to the big city until next winter." He grins at his own joke, offers us a salute and prepares to continue on his way.

But Mom steps into his path. "Not so fast, hotshot," she growls. "I've got a bone to pick with you."

He takes a step back, and his eyebrows shoot up. He's clearly not accustomed to being called out—at least, not by a woman. I find that surprising. From what I've seen of the guy, I'm guessing he ticks people off on a regular basis.

He clearly knows what Mom is talking about, though, because he nods and looks away. "You're mad about me for passing you on Round Lake," he says. "I know I shouldn't have done it, but it was sort of an emergency."

Aha! That's what I'd said.

"An emergency? Uh-huh." Mom's tone says she's more than a little skeptical. "Care to elaborate? As I recall, you were hauling lumber. Was there midnight construction planned for something?"

He ignores the sarcasm. "At the last minute I was asked to pick up a part for the school furnace. They've been out of heat for a couple of days already, and even though there are no classes right now, they were worried about the pipes freezing. I was supposed to be in Pauingassi by dinnertime, but I was held up in Bloodvein, waiting for the part."

"That doesn't excuse your reckless driving on the lake," Mom says, though I notice there's not as much venom in her tone as before. "Do you realize you caused an ice wave?"

From the expression on Dwayne's face, I'm guessing he didn't. "Seriously?" he sputters. "Oh my god. I'm so sorry. I didn't know. Really. I never thought—"

"That's the problem," Mom says, refusing to cut him any slack. "You didn't think. Maybe you should start. You're not the only one driving these roads, you know. Risk your own life all you want, but don't take the rest of us down with you. My daughter was in my truck!"

"I'm really, really sorry," he says again. "Really."

"Right." Mom is clearly unconvinced.

Message sent, we carry on to the store. When we come out again, Dwayne and his semi are gone, and the unloading of the truck begins. While the storekeeper waves his arms and shouts directions, Mom passes boxes down to a couple of guys who've been recruited to move them inside. Most of the cartons contain food, cleaning supplies and paper products. But there are some medical supplies too—first-aid stuff, headache tablets, cold and flu remedies—that sort of thing. As I watch the parade of boxes moving from truck to store, I can't help thinking of the semi as a giant cornucopia. No matter how many trips the guys make, it still seems full.

But then I think about how long these supplies have to last, and I start to wonder if the community will have enough to get them through the rest of the winter. It could be weeks—maybe months—before planes will be able to bring in anything. During that time, Pauingassi and Little Grand Rapids will be completely isolated.

Knowing I'm going to be cooped up in the semi all day, I want to stay mobile as long as I can, so I tag along behind Mom as she and the storekeeper head inside to deal with the paperwork.

"Are you heading back to Winnipeg?" he asks Mom.

"Yup," she replies. "This is a quick trip. I have to pick up another load tomorrow morning."

"Well, good luck to you," the store-keeper says. "The forecast is for record high temps today. If this weather keeps up, the road won't be safe for longer than two or three more days. At this rate, we might not see you again until next year."

"Will that work for you?" Mom asks.

He grins. "It might have to."

As Mom and I head onto the road again, I'm caught up in my thoughts. First, I'm amazed at how the people who live here survive. It takes a brand of guts and determination I'm not sure I have. Second, I'm impressed by the truckers who travel the dangerous winter roads, because they are the only lifeline communities such as Pauingassi and Little Grand Rapids have. Without truckers like my mom, life here wouldn't be possible.

Chapter Nine

The winter road looks completely different by day. Last night, all I could see was the ribbon of packed snow illuminated by the semi's headlights. Other than that, the world was a suffocating black. But now trees rise up around us on every side, dwarfing the skinny man-made trail and making me more aware than ever that we are in the wilderness, and Mother Nature is in control.

"Do you ever get nervous driving the winter roads?" I ask my mother.

"I'm respectful of them," she says, "but I'm also prepared. So no, I'm not usually nervous. If I had truck trouble I couldn't fix, or if I was caught in a storm, I'd be fine until another vehicle came along. Remote as the area is, it still gets traffic."

I point to the remains of a rusted camper in the trees off to the side. "Looks like not everyone makes it out."

Mom shakes her head and clucks her tongue. "Some people use the winter roads to get rid of derelict cars, rotting boats and other trash."

"The wilderness isn't a garbage dump."

"Unfortunately, not everyone thinks that way."

"Why don't they get arrested or fined?"

"The authorities have to catch them first, and there just isn't the manpower. But all that's going to change. The government is in the process of building permanent roads and bridges to link all the remote communities in the province. Increased traffic should help cut down on illegal dumping."

"You mean they're building honest-to-goodness real roads?"

She nods. "Yes. Within the next twenty-five years, the ice and snow roads in Manitoba will be a thing of the past. And that's a good thing."

"What's that?" I sit up and point to a splotch of red in the middle of the road. As we get closer, I can see a smear of red leading away from the main stain and ending beside a brown mound on Mom's side of the truck.

"Dead deer," she says. "My guess is it had a run-in with a vehicle—and lost. Not that long ago either."

We exchange looks, and although I'm pretty sure we're both thinking the same thing, neither of us says a word. We haven't passed any vehicles since leaving Pauingassi, and there was only one heading out on the road before us—a shiny red semi.

Deer get hit by cars and trucks every day. They dart out of the bush and onto the road before drivers can react. I know that. And yet I'm not willing to give Dwayne Bradley the benefit of the doubt. In my mind, his recklessness is what killed the deer. The guy only cares about himself. So I'm a bit concerned that Mom and I have to drive behind him. If he's speeding, he could chew the winter road to bits, and that would not be good news for us. I'm especially worried about the damage he might do to Round Lake. If he breaks the ice before we get there, we'll be stranded.

"I can't believe how hot it is." I fan myself and peel off my jacket.

Mom adjusts the heat in the cab. "The forecast is for a high of fifteen today. That's really warm for mid-March. If this mini heat wave continues, the winter roads will shut down. I'm glad we're heading home."

As we pass Little Grand Rapids, we see Harvey and Finn fueling up their semi, getting ready to head out. Mom lays on the horn. They look up, smile and wave. I wave too and then sigh and lean back in my seat. So much for getting to know Finn. I'll probably never see him again.

The return drive is pretty uneventful, which is fine with me. The sun is shining, and Mom and I are gabbing and laughing as we make our way back toward Bloodvein. At lunchtime, we park in a pull-off and eat. Things between us feel more like they used to, and I'm happier than I've been since before my dad died.

The sun is already low and has lost its heat by the time we reach Round Lake. Considering that Dwayne got here ahead of us, I half expect to see broken ice floating haphazardly over the surface of the lake. I imagine Mom and me abandoning the truck and hopping across the floes to reach the other side. I don't share this thought with my mother though. Actually, the ice looks as solid as it did when we drove across it last night. Even so, I undo my seat belt and hang on to the door handle.

"We're making good time," Mom says as she eases the semi onto the lake. "At this rate we could be home at a reasonable hour."

The ice groans and creaks beneath the truck's weight.

"Are you sure it's safe?" I ask, my nose pressed against the side window. "It was pretty hot today."

Mom smiles. "It's fine, Kat. Don't worry. It takes more than a couple of warm days to melt the ice."

"If you say so," I concede, though I continue to study the lake for cracks.

We ride in silence for about five minutes, and then Mom mumbles, "What the…"

I look out the front window and gasp. Up ahead, sitting sideways on the ice road with its grill pushed into the far snowbank, is Dwayne's semi.

"He must have lost control," I say.

"The way he's been driving, I wouldn't be surprised," Mom grumbles. "That guy is a menace on the road. First the ice wave, then the deer, and now this. I've had it with him. When we get back to Winnipeg, I'm calling the authorities." She slows down so much, we're barely moving. "Can you see him?" she asks me.

I squint into the dying light, trying to see around and under the semi. I shake my head. "No. What if he's hurt?"

"There's only one way to find out. As much as I'd like to kick the little jerk in his sorry butt, we can't leave him here if he's in trouble." She heaves a heavy sigh. Then she slips the truck into neutral and sets the brake.

"I thought you weren't supposed to stop on an ice road," I remind her.

She hops out and looks across the cab at me. "Well, I don't really have a choice, do I? But it should be fine. I'm parked a safe distance from his rig, and I'm not hauling anything. Neither is he, so weight shouldn't be a problem. Stay here. I'll be right back."

Should be fine? Shouldn't be a problem? Yeah right, Mom. Until the truck plunges through the ice and I end up at the bottom of the lake. I jump down from my side of the cab and run after her.

She frowns at me when I catch up. "I told you to stay in the truck."

I'm not about to admit I'm too paranoid to do that, so I say, "Considering your frame of mind, I thought you might need a referee. Since I don't know how to drive the semi out of here, I can't risk you and Dwayne killing each other."

She rolls her eyes and keeps walking. "Dwayne," she calls as we near his vehicle. It's still running. "Where are you? Are you okay?" She gestures for me to head around to the passenger side of the truck while she jogs toward the driver's side.

There's no sign of him, so I walk to the front of the cab, where the grill is mashed into the snowbank. He's not there either. I scan the road and the snow-covered lake beyond. If he went out there and fell, we'll never find him.

Mom calls his name again and bangs on the cab, so I hurry around to the other side of the truck, arriving just as she yanks the door open and steps up onto the running board.

"Oh god," she says in a voice that sends dread shooting through me.

"What? What's wrong?"

She climbs into the cab without answering. I jump onto the running board and peer inside. Lying on the floor between the seats—half in the front and half in the back—is Dwayne. He isn't moving. Mom is wedged between the dashboard and the passenger seat. Her fingers are searching his neck for a pulse.

I hold my breath and wait.

Chapter Ten

"He's alive," Mom says, "but his pulse is slow."

"Maybe he got knocked out when the semi hit the snowbank," I suggest.

She looks skeptical. "I don't think so. There's no blood and no bumps or bruises. But he's soaked in sweat. That says sick to me. I have a feeling he passed out *before* the semi hit the snowbank."

"So what do we do?"

"I'll radio the RCMP and tell them the situation. I think he needs a doctor."

"Should we get him off the floor?" I ask. "It can't be very comfortable. And it's probably cold. We could pull the bed down and put him on that."

She shakes her head. "There's not much room to maneuver him, plus he's a dead weight. I don't think we could lift him. We'd probably do him more harm than good. We should cover him up though. You find a blanket while I radio for help."

While Mom steps over Dwayne to get back to the driver's seat and the CB, I climb into the back of the cab.

I pull down the bunk folded against the back wall of the cab and rip the blanket off the mattress. Then I tuck it around Dwayne. I can't believe how pale he is and how still—he's barely breathing. I've never been in a situation like this before. I wasn't even around when my dad died, so it feels kind of surreal. I have to keep reminding myself that this isn't my imagination or a television program. This is really happening, and what Mom and I do could make a huge difference in how things turn out. I can't say I like Dwayne much, but I don't want anything bad to happen to him either.

Mom is still talking on the radio when I'm done, so I start pulling open cupboards, looking for—I don't know—something. And *bingo!* There on the first shelf is a box of insulin pens. Somebody else might not recognize them, but I do.

"Mom!" I shout.

She spins toward me, frowning.

"Look!" I shake the pens at her. "It's insulin. Dwayne must be a diabetic. Maybe that's why he passed out."

Mom instantly relays my discovery to the person on the other end of the radio. "Hang on. I'll check," she says and leans over Dwayne, pulling back the cuffs of his jacket. Then she's back on the CB. "No. No medical-alert bracelet."

Without thinking, I twist mine on my wrist.

"Any sign of seizure?" I can barely make out the voice on the radio over the static.

"No," Mom says.

"Is there any indication that he's eaten recently?"

As Mom checks the front of the cab, I pull open the fridge and cupboards in the back.

"Nothing here, "I say, "except for a couple of bottles of water and an unopened box of granola bars."

"No," Mom says into the radio. "There's half a thermos of coffee, but that's it."

"Has he regained consciousness at all?" the person asks.

Mom glances at Dwayne. "No. He was out when we discovered him a little over five minutes ago, and he hasn't moved while we've been here."

"If he's not on his side, turn him. We need to make sure his airways are open," the dispatcher says, so Mom and I get to work.

"Ooh," I say, as I catch a whiff of his breath. "He smells like he's been drinking."

Mom repeats what I've said into the radio.

"Classic symptom of low blood sugar," the dispatcher replies, "though there's no way of knowing for sure until we check his levels."

Without even thinking, I grab the handset. "I could check his sugar levels. I'm a diabetic too. I use a glucose meter all the time."

"What?" The dispatcher sounds confused.

Mom takes the handset from me. "That was my daughter," she explains. "And she's right. She could check his sugar levels."

"Do it then," the person says "and radio us the results. If you're on Round Lake, it's going to take too long for you to get him to us, so we'll send a chopper. Stay near the radio."

Though Dwayne probably has a glucose meter somewhere in his semi, I have no idea where. I could hunt for it, but it's probably faster to get my own, so I race back to our truck. I'm not gone more than five minutes, but I'm puffing as I climb back into the semi.

After six months of living with diabetes, using the machine has become second nature, and I don't waste a second getting to work.

"It's showing 2.6," I tell Mom once I've transferred the blood drop from

Dwayne's finger to the glucose strip. "That's really low."

As Mom radios in the reading, headlights appear in the distance from the direction of Little Grand Rapids. It's another big truck. It stops behind Mom's semi, though not too close. As I squint into the darkness, two silhouettes, backlit by the headlights, run down the lake toward us. As they get closer, I can see they are men, and one of them is really tall. It can only be Harvey and Finn.

Before Mom can open the window to tell them what's happening, they're caught in a puddle of light. They both shield their eyes and look up. I open the door on my side of the semi, step onto the running board and stare skyward too. I half expect to see an alien space-ship dragging Harvey and Finn aboard with a tractor beam. But there's no spaceship—just a helicopter. Talk about losing my grip on reality. The situation with Dwayne has me more stressed than I realized. I jump down from the truck. With the arrival of the paramedics, I feel like the weight of the world has been lifted from my shoulders.

The helicopter lands farther up the lake. I guess it doesn't want to concentrate any more weight in the immediate area. It seems everyone who lives or works in this part of Manitoba is respectful of the winter roads.

As soon as the chopper touches down, two men jump out with a stretcher and hurry toward us. Finn and I stand out of the way as the pilot and paramedic—with Harvey's help—maneuver Dwayne out of the truck. Then they immediately head back to the helicopter, with Mom and Harvey running alongside, answering questions.

"Well, this sure isn't an average day on the winter road," Finn yells. Even from a distance, the helicopter is noisy.

"No kidding," I yell back. "Dwayne is in pretty rough shape. I hope he's going to be okay."

Finn nods. "I had no clue he was a diabetic."

"Why would you?" I reply. "It's not something that shows on the outside. Mostly, if you eat right, take your insulin and control your sugar levels, you can live like everybody else." Part of me can't believe what I'm saying. I sound like my mother.

"How do you know so much about it?" Finn asks.

I shrug. "It takes one to know one." I can't believe I said that either. I don't usually tell people I have diabetes. I'm afraid they'll treat me like a freak or an invalid. For a few seconds, Finn doesn't answer. He just stares at me, and I start to wonder if I've scared him off. But then—

"So I guess asking if I can take you out for a Coke next time I'm in Winnipeg isn't such a good idea," he says.

Though I'd been hoping for a chance to see Finn again, his suggestion still comes as a surprise. I smile self-consciously. "Oh, I don't know. It's not such a terrible idea. I can always have tea."

He shrugs. "That could work too. So can I have your number?"

Chapter Eleven

As the chopper takes off, the four of us watch, squinting through the wind it has stirred up. It's stronger than I would have thought, and I have to grab on to Finn and Mom to keep from flying off into the night with the helicopter.

"So here's the plan," Harvey says when the chopper is finally on its way. "We'll convoy our way back to the highway. I'll drive Dwayne's rig and leave it in Winnipeg with the company he's driving for. They can figure out how to get it to him. Finn, you drive our truck and pick me up. And ladies, you keep us steady through the middle."

Mom nods. "Sounds good. The sooner we're off this ice road, the happier I'll be. My truck's been sitting in one spot with its engine running way too long. Let's get this parade moving."

As we jog off to our trucks, we wave and call our goodbyes.

Mom pulls forward by a truck length and then sticks the semi back into neutral, while Harvey frees the nose of Dwayne's rig from the snow-bank and repositions the semi on the ice. A blast from his horn signals he's ready, and he moves forward. Mom and Finn reply with horn blasts of their own and fall in behind him. Ten minutes later we're off Round Lake and back on the snow road.

My frazzled nerves uncurl a bit. Not that the snow road isn't treacherous too, but if it crumbles, we're not going to end up at the bottom of a lake. We'll merely be stuck in the middle of nowhere at the mercy of the elements and wild animals. Definitely the more preferable option.

"How far behind schedule are you?" I ask my mom. "Will you still be able to connect with the next shipment?"

"We were on Round Lake for over an hour. That means a bit less sleep, but I should be fine for tomorrow." She smiles, but I can see the strain on her face. We still have a long drive ahead, and she's already tired. Clearly, the situation with Dwayne has taken its toll. Suddenly I feel guilty. If I was spooked seeing Dwayne unconscious and helpless, my mother is ten times more rattled. I have a feeling it was me she imagined lying on the floor of the truck.

"Do you think he's going to be okay?" I say.

"The paramedic said they'd let us know."

I nod. Though I am concerned about Dwayne, I can't stop thinking, That could have been me. From the day I was first diagnosed, part of me has been denying my condition. Stupid as it sounds, I've wanted to blame my mother—not like she made the diabetes happen, but that by making it the center of my life and forcing me to follow the rules to the letter, she's made it worse. I don't feel horrible, so how can I be sick? But seeing what happened to Dwayne, I think it's finally starting to sink in. I feel okay, because my mom is on top of things. She doesn't let a single thing slide. I didn't realize how important that was until now. And with everything else she has on her plate, I'm starting to feel guilty about dumping that burden on her.

I'm the one with diabetes, so it's my job to deal with it. It's time I faced up to that.

The winter road is closed two days later. Lucky for my mother, her next run is highway driving only.

This time, she lets me stay home by myself. I don't even have to plead. In fact, she's the one who suggests it. She leaves all the appropriate emergency numbers, phones me several times a day and arranges for Tina to check in on me, but otherwise I'm on my own. It's only for three days, but it's Mom showing faith in me, and me getting a chance to prove I deserve her trust.

Mom and Gran arrive home on the same day, and to my surprise, neither of them rushes to check my insulin and sugar-level readings. I am obviously still alive and well, and though I'm sure they're curious, they don't let on.

I make dinner, setting the table extra special. I stick to Mom's menus, but maybe because I'm the one doing the cooking, everything seems more appetizing. I can hardly wait to serve up my "masterpiece."

The doorbell rings just as I'm about to do so.

"Company?" Mom asks.

Gran shrugs. "No one I know."

"Don't look at me," I say. "I didn't invite anyone."

Mom and I open the front door together and blink in disbelief. Standing on our porch is Dwayne Bradley. Mom is first to shake off her surprise.

"Dwayne!" She opens the door wide and smiles. "Come in. Come in. It's so good to see you back on your feet. You had us all pretty scared there for a while."

He hangs his head sheepishly and shuffles inside. "Yeah. I'm really sorry about that. That's why I came round. I got your address from your dispatcher. I hope that's okay. I could've phoned or sent a card, but you guys saved my life. That's huge, and I needed to thank you in person." He offers us a nervous smile.

Mom squeezes his arm. "We're just glad you're up and about again. So come and sit down and tell us how you're doing." She pulls him into the living room. I follow behind and sit beside my grandmother.

"I'm a lot better," Dwayne says. "I only found out I have diabetes a couple of months ago. I guess I didn't want to believe it. I never really listened to the doctor or nurses at the clinic when they were explaining things. I figured if I took the insulin, that would be good enough." He pauses and shakes his head. "Obviously it isn't."

"Well, now you know, and that's the important thing," Mom tells him.

"You can't expect to adapt to something like diabetes overnight. It takes time."

I enter the conversation for the first time. "My mom's right. I haven't had diabetes long either—only about six months—and I'm still wrapping my head around it. What you need is a support system. The Diabetes Information Center is a great place to start. They help you understand what's going on with your body, they regulate your medication, and they teach you how to make sense of your glucose readings. And they're always there to answer any questions."

He nods. "Yeah, since I got out of the hospital, I've been going there. They've already helped me a lot. I'm taking some time off driving, until I get a handle on things. My parents have been great. I'm back home with them for the time being." He smiles and rolls his eyes. "My mom has made it her personal mission to see that I eat right."

I lean forward and whisper behind my hand, "Moms are like that."

Of course, Mom hears me, and we all laugh. "Hold on a minute," she objects. "Who made dinner tonight? It wasn't me."

Dwayne instantly jumps to his feet. "Oh gosh, I'm sorry. I'm keeping you from your supper."

"Yes, you are," I agree, ignoring the disapproving glare from my mother. "And that's not a good thing, since we diabetics need to eat regularly. That means you too, Dwayne, so you are officially invited to dinner. We can't risk having you pass out again. I'll set another place."

Before Dwayne can argue, I jump up and head for the kitchen. Halfway there, I hear my phone ring. I spin around to retrieve it from the coffee table, but Mom already has it in her hand. She looks at the screen and then raises an eyebrow as she holds the phone out to me.

"It's Finn," she says. "Now where do you suppose he got your number?"

I shake my head and assume a puzzled expression. "Huh. I wonder." But when I take the phone from my mom, I can't help smiling.

"Katarina Mulholland," Mom growls sternly.

I give her a peck on the cheek. "Love you, Mom." Then I swing the phone up to my ear and race for the privacy of the kitchen.

ACKNOWLEDGMENTS

Never before have I attempted a novel on subjects I know so little about—diabetes, trucking and winter roads. Though I had the interest, I lacked the knowledge. Consequently, I spent as much time researching as writing. Though the Internet became my best friend, I tapped other sources as well. My doctor, my daughter and my pharmacist let me pick their brains about the various aspects of diabetes. For the trucking facet of the story, I watched more videos than I can count. Did you know you can learn how to do just about anything on YouTube? Initially my husband helped me with the winter roads, since he had traveled them back in the 1980s. But that was over thirty years ago, and it soon became evident that I needed more current information. Enter Tim Smyrski, the Winter Road Program manager for Manitoba. Tim went out of his way to answer all my questions, map a route for my story, provide interesting details and even send me pictures of the roads. Many thanks to him and to everyone else who contributed to this novel. I could never have managed it without you.

Kristin Butcher is the author of many books for young people, including *Alibi* and *Cabin Girl* in the Orca Currents series. She taught a variety of subjects, from primary to high-school level, before becoming an author. She has always had a wild imagination and is pretty sure she'll never run out of ideas for stories. Kristin lives in Campbell River, British Columbia. For more information, visit www.kristinbutcher.com.